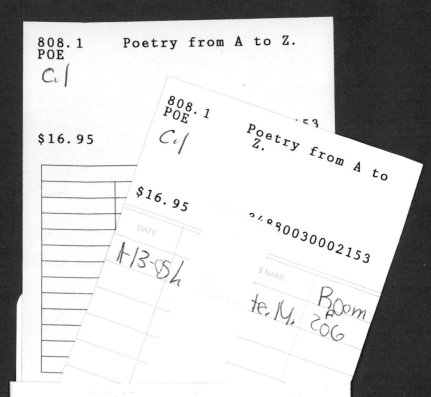

808.1   Poetry from A to Z.
POE
Cı

$16.95

808.1   53
POE
Cı

$16.95

DATE   Poetry from A to
                              Z.
1-13-04
                         34880030002153

                         NAME
te. M.   Room
           206

BAKER & TAYLOR

Also by Paul B. Janeczko

POETRY COLLECTIONS

Strings: A Gathering of Family Poems

Pocket Poems

Poetspeak: In Their Work, About Their Work

Dont Forget to Fly

Postcard Poems

Going Over to Your Place: Poems for Each Other

This Delicious Day: 65 Poems

The Music of What Happens:
Poems That Tell Stories

The Place My Words Are Looking For

Preposterous: Poems of Youth

Looking for Your Name

•

ORIGINAL POETRY

Brickyard Summer

Stardust Otel

•

FICTION

Bridges to Cross

•

NONFICTION

Loads of Codes and Secret Ciphers

POETRY
from
A *to* Z

A Guide for Young Writers

Compiled by **Paul B. Janeczko**

Illustrated by **Cathy Bobak**

Simon & Schuster Books for Young Readers

SIMON & SCHUSTER BOOKS FOR YOUNG READERS
An imprint of Simon & Schuster Children's Publishing Division
1230 Avenue of the Americas, New York, New York 10020

Simon & Schuster Books for Young Readers is a trademark of Simon & Schuster

Text copyright © 1994 by Paul B. Janeczko
Illustrations copyright © 1994 by Cathy Bobak

Pages 117-121 constitute an extension of the copyright page.
The text of this book is set Cheltenham Light.
Book design by Cathy Bobak

10   9
Printed and bound in the United States of America

Library of Congress Cataloging-in-Publication Data
Poetry from A to Z : a guide for young writers /
selected by Paul B. Janeczko ; illustrated by Cathy Bobak. — 1st ed.
p.   cm.
Includes bibliographical references and index.
ISBN 0-02-747672-3
1. Poetry—Authorship—Juvenile literature.   2. Authorship—
Juvenile literature.   [1. Poetry—Authorship.   2. Authorship.   3. American
poetry—Collections.]   I. Janeczko, Paul B.   II. Bobak, Cathy, ill.
PN145.P56   1994
808.1—dc20   94-10528

for Richard Moore
who loves books
who bleeds Dodger blue

CONTENTS

Introduction

It's no exaggeration to say that poetry changed my life. It's helped me to see, feel, and think in new ways. Yet when I was a kid, I didn't care for poetry. I didn't read it unless I had to. I would rather take out the trash or visit a cranky uncle who smelled like my attic. I would have never thought of picking up a book like this. Writing poetry seemed a mysteriously impossible task for me and my friends.

I'm not sure how that all changed. I wish I knew whom to thank for opening the door to poetry. I suspect there was more than one person responsible for showing me the outrageous joy of reading and writing poems.

Poetry writing doesn't cost much. A cheap pen and a notebook are all you need to get started. And, unless you write an unkind poem about a bully who made you eat dirty snow, it's not hazardous to your health. You don't need anybody else to write poetry, although it's always nice to share your poems with friends and family.

This book is a guide. It's not going to tell you all there is to know about poetry. But it *is* going to offer

1

you some good ideas to get you started writing poems. *Poetry from A to Z* contains seventy-two poems that can serve as models for you. They are arranged alphabetically by subject or theme to show you that you can write a poem about almost anything. In addition to the poems, I've included fourteen poetry-writing exercises that show you how to write specific types of poems, like an acrostic or a persona poem. Finally, twenty-three poets whose works are in this book have offered helpful advice on becoming a better poet.

Don't be afraid to try to write poems like those in this book. As you gain more confidence in your own writing, you will imitate other poets less and less. The poems were chosen and arranged from A to Z to help you see that you can write poems about nearly any subject, so don't hesitate to write a poem just because your topic seems weird. At the same time, even though somebody's already written a poem about what you'd like to write about, you should still try to write your poem because it will likely be different.

Writing a poem isn't like building a model of a ship, using carefully numbered plans to assemble so many perfectly fitting pieces. It's more like building a tree house in the woods or a hideout in the far corner of a vacant lot. It takes time to build a good tree house (or a good poem): time to observe and decide what you'd like your tree house to look like; time to remember other tree houses you've seen; time to build; and time to change it if something doesn't work out or you find something new to add that will make your tree house better.

You need the right tools. As a young writer, you should include in your toolbox a few pens, pencils, and markers that feel comfortable in your hand. I like to write with a fountain pen. Other poets use a felt-tip marker or a No. 2 pencil lined with their teeth marks. You'll also need a notebook where you can keep all your ideas and poems. Make it a thick one so you won't be afraid to use a few pages when you rewrite a poem. It will be helpful if you have a dictionary, a thesaurus, and a rhyming dictionary nearby. Each book is packed with great words that can improve your poems.

In addition to the concrete things in your toolbox, you'll need ideas and feelings to write about. They come from observing and listening and living (and jotting the interesting things in your notebook). I'm sure you've had some interesting experiences so far in your life—some happy, some not, but surely experiences that you'd like to write about. Those experiences and observations are what you should save in your notebook and write poems about.

Do you have a good place to write? That's important. Maybe you have your own room. Or maybe you have your special place away from home. Do you like to write curled up in a bumpy old stuffed chair near the window? In the kitchen while your father feeds the baby? Some writers need absolute silence to write. Others, like me, can write while they have music playing. Do what works for you.

When you write a poem that you like, don't keep it to yourself. Poetry should be shared. Jot your poem on a postcard and mail it to a friend or relative. (Or mail it to me at the publisher's address.) Write it on a sheet of pretty paper and slip it to someone special. I know that sharing your poems may be difficult at first. But as you feel more confident about your writing, you'll find it easier to share your poems.

One more thing. Don't be afraid to experiment. If you want to write a poem that's not quite like any of the ones in this book, try it! Over the years, poets—Walt Whitman, Emily Dickinson, e. e. cummings, to name but a few—have experimented with form, meter, language. Without such experiments, poetry would never have grown the way it has. If your poem doesn't work out the way you thought it would, try to fix it. If the poem refuses to come out the way you want it, try something different.

One of the great things about writing poetry is that

you can write whatever you like. You can also change it as many times as you want. Keep that in mind as you write your poems. Work and play with the words until you get them just right. A poem is finished when you are satisfied with it.

Autumn Beat
Monica Kulling

leaves
are racing
down
the street

bundled
bunches
at my
feet

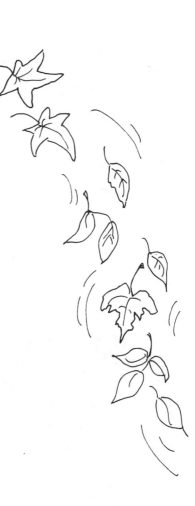

a scrunch
a crunch
a dry, bright
sound

I shuffle
scuffle
into town

Try This: Acrostic Poem

Acrostic poems don't rhyme. But they do try to use a few right words to tell a story or describe someone. Each line of an acrostic poem begins with one letter in the title/subject of the poem. In other words, the first letter of each line will spell the title. Here are a few examples:

DANIEL

Does not
Allow any
Nagging or
Insults to get to him.
Everyone
Likes his big eyes.

SISTER

She
Is always
Sharing her
Time with me.
Even though she's
Rather weird.

PJ (our dog)

Practices
Jumping over cats.

If you have a problem thinking of somebody to write about, start with the members of your family. I bet you have something to say about *them*! Don't forget your friends. They make wonderful subjects for acrostic poems.

Start by writing the name of your subject at the top of the page. Then try to think of the most important things to say about that person. Don't try to say *everything* about that person. You can't do it in such a short poem. As you come up with good ideas, try them out on paper. Don't forget that the first letter of each line must come from the title/subject of the poem.

You can also write acrostic poems about abstract ideas, like love, beauty, and loneliness. Of course, this type of poem is more challenging to write than the ones about people, but it's worth the effort. As with any good poem, it's important to include concrete details that allow the reader to see and feel what the poet saw and felt.

I said earlier that acrostic poems don't rhyme. However, that shouldn't stop you from experimenting with rhyme when you write your acrostics. Once you understand how to write a particular type of poem, feel free to try some variations.

Bird Watcher
Jane Yolen

Across the earless
face of the moon
a stretch of Vs
honks homeward.
From the lake
laughs the last joke
of a solitary loon.
Winter silences us all.
I will miss
these conversations,
the trips at dawn
and dusk,
where I listen carefully,
then answer
only with my eyes.

I will have a single line running through my head and
that will be the start of a poem. It may not be the first
line, but it will be the beginning.   —Jane Yolen

Try This: Blessing and Prayer Poems

One way to look at prayer and blessing poems is to see them as the opposite of curse poems (page 21). Where a curse is meant to call unpleasantness on somebody or something, a prayer or a blessing is meant to request protection or good fortune for a subject. Patricia Hubbell does this in her poem "Prayer for Reptiles":

> God, keep all claw-denned alligators
> Free.
> Keep snake and lizard, tortoise, toad,
> All creep-crawl
> Tip-toe turtles
> Where they stand,
> Keep these;
> All smile-mouthed crocodiles,
> Young taut-skinned, sun-wet
> Creatures of the sea,
> Thin, indecisive hoppers
> Of the shore,
> Keep these;
> All hurt, haunt, hungry
> Reptiles
> Wandering the marge,
> All land-confused
> Amphibians,

Sea-driven,
Keep these;
Keep snakes, toads, lizards,
All hop, all crawl, all climb,
Keep these,
Keep these.

Although a prayer and a blessing may be the opposite of a curse, you can write them the same way you write a curse. You can start your lines with *May* or *Let*. Also, these poems have some of the qualities of a list poem (page 62), so your poem may include a number of things that you want protected or blessed.

The subjects of your prayer and blessing poems are people or things that are dear to you. Perhaps you want to write about your friends or family or prized possessions, mentioning each one individually and including some special wish for each one. If you're concerned about the earth, maybe your prayer will be like "Prayer for Reptiles." A special environmental concern—endangered species, the rain forest, rivers and lakes—might make a good poem. A good prayer poem might be for your best friend, including specific reasons why he/she should be blessed.

If you'd like to read another blessing/prayer poem, turn to "Prayer for Fish" by Ronald Wallace (page 80).

B B B B B B B B B B B B B

BUILDING
Gwendolyn Brooks

When I see a brave building
straining high, and higher,
hard and bright and sassy in the seasons,
I think of the hands that put that strength together.

The little soft hands. Hands coming away from cold
to take a challenge and to mold this definition.

Amazingly, men and women
worked with design and judgment, steel and glass,
to enact this announcement.
Here it stands.

Who can construct such miracle can enact
any consolidation, any fusion.
All little people opening out of themselves,

forging the human spirit that can outwit
big Building boasting in the cityworld.

Be yourself. Don't imitate other poets. *You* are as
important as *they* are. —Gwendolyn Brooks

Try This: Clerihew

Clerihews were invented by E. C. Bentley in 1890, when he was a schoolboy. They were later popularized in a column he wrote for a London newspaper. Bentley created a poem of two couplets that poked gentle fun at politicians, movie stars, historical figures. And he named it after himself; his middle name was Clerihew. (Well, if you invented a poem, wouldn't *you* name it after yourself? I know I would.)

There are a few things to keep in mind when you try to write a clerihew. First of all, a clerihew is about a celebrity, and the point of the poem is to poke *gentle fun* at the subject. The celebrity's name must end the first line, and, since the poem is made up of two couplets, you must rhyme with that name (a couplet is two lines that rhyme). The first line of a true clerihew contains only the name of the subject. However, if you wish, you may identify your subject with a few words prior to her/his name. For example:

That famous lady, Mona Lisa
Whose smile has been a teaser
Will never tell this world we're in
What's behind that fabled grin.

Or:

Basketball ace, Dr. J.
Is seven feet tall they say
His only hang-up is buying shoes.
That's why they had to invent canoes.

When you think of writing a clerihew, you may know immediately whom you'd like to write about—maybe your favorite soap opera star or rock musician. If you have trouble coming up with a subject, jot down a list of celebrity categories. Here are some examples: musicians, movie stars, TV stars, characters in books, cartoon characters. Once you have your list, it might be easier for you to think of a specific person to write about. The next thing you need to decide is what aspect of that person you want to base your poem on. You might want to write about President Clinton's saxophone playing.

Once you start writing your clerihew, keep the lines short, something between seven and nine syllables per line. And don't forget that you must rhyme with the subject's name.

CONCRETE MIXERS
Patricia Hubbell

The drivers are washing the concrete mixers;
Like elephant tenders they hose them down.
Tough grey-skinned monsters standing ponderous,
Elephant-bellied and elephant-nosed,
Standing in muck up to their wheel-caps,
Like rows of elephants, tail to trunk.
Their drivers perch on their backs like mahouts,
Sending the sprays of water up.
They rid the trunk-like trough of concrete,
Direct the spray to the bulging sides,
Turn and start the monsters moving.

      Concrete mixers
      Move like elephants
      Bellow like elephants
      Spray like elephants,
Concrete mixers are urban elephants,
Their trunks are raising a city.

c c c c c c c c c c c c c

To write poetry, you must be like an athlete—alert but relaxed, paying attention to everything going on around you. That way, poetry subjects won't escape your notice. When you write, let your thoughts go where they will. The ending of your poem may turn out to be a big surprise!   —Patricia Hubbell

White Cat
Raymond Knister

I like to go to the stable after supper,–
Remembering fried potatoes and tarts of snow-apple jam–
And watch the men curry the horses,
And feed the pigs, and especially give the butting calves their
     milk.
When my father has finished milking he will say,
"Now Howard, you'll have to help me carry in these pails.
How will your mother be getting along
All this time without her little man?"
So we go in, and he carries them, but I help.
My father and I don't need the lanterns.
They hang on the wires up high back of the stalls
And we leave them for Ern and Dick.
It seems such a long way to the house in the dark,

But sometimes we talk, and always
There's the White Cat, that has been watching
While my father milked.
In the dark its gallop goes before like air,
Without any noise,
And it thinks we're awfully slow
Coming with the milk.

MOON
William Jay Smith

I have a white cat whose name is Moon;
He eats catfish from a wooden spoon,
And sleeps till five each afternoon.

Moon goes out when the moon is bright
And sycamore trees are spotted white
To sit and stare in the dead of night.

Beyond still water cries a loon,
Through mulberry leaves peers a wild baboon,
And in Moon's eyes I see the moon.

C C C C C C C C C C C C C

Try This: Curse Poem

One day I wrote a poem because I was very upset with somebody. I can't even remember who it was. It could have been the person in the car in front of me who was driving too slowly when I was in a hurry. Or it could have been a thing that upset me. Maybe the trash bag that broke while I was carrying it to the back door. More than likely, however, a number of things were bothering me, and the poem was my way of dealing with them all. When I'd completed the poem, I laughed at the silly things I had been upset with. And I laughed at the harmless curses I included in the poem. I called my poem "If I Could Put a Curse on You":

> If I could put a curse on you
> I would have a laugh or two
>
> May your gym shorts drop below your knees
> May your locker fill with killer bees
>
> May you bust the spokes on your new bike
> May your girlfriend tell you "Take a hike!"
>
> May you foul the science on the test
> May you skulk around the halls half dressed

May your parents find out what you did
May the bully find out where you hid

May your lunch get purloined and eaten
May your favorite team get beaten

May you get a pimple on your nose
May you grow an extra pair of toes

Oh, if I could put a curse on you
I would have a laugh or two

But only someone who's a brat
Would do a rotten thing like that.

If you want to write a curse poem, you can model your poem after mine, which is made up of couplets (two lines that rhyme). Most of the lines—the lines that actually contain the curses—begin with *May*. My poem has six couplets of curses, but there's no special reason for that. You can write a poem with fewer lines, if you wish. Or more, if you have a lot to say.

It's important to remember that writing this poem is supposed to be fun, so make sure that your curses are silly or harmless. One way to get a laugh with your curses is to exaggerate like I did: "May you grow an extra pair of toes," or "May your locker fill with killer bees." You can make your curses those harmless things that drive us crazy: "May you get a pimple on your nose," or "May your favorite team get beaten." There's plenty of violence and hurt and nastiness in the world already without our adding to it, so write a poem that gets a laugh because it's goofy and wild.

This is one of the poems in this book that has a consistent rhythm. All good poems have rhythm. In some poems rhythm will be more obvious than it is in others. Just as you can hear and feel the rhythm of a clock ticking or a train passing in front of the family car, you can hear and feel the rhythm in poetry. If you listen to the train too long, it will get boring because it's too much of one rhythm. The same thing happens in poetry if the poet does not vary the rhythm of his/her poems.

I Picked a Dream Out of My Head
John Ciardi

I picked a dream out of my head
When I was fast asleep.
It was about a fish that said,
"I am too small to keep!"

I threw it back and tried again.
That time I dreamed a yak
That said to me, "It looks like rain:
I'd best be starting back!"

I picked another one about
A tiger in a top hat.
It snarled so that I had to shout,
"This is my dream: you stop that!"

There was one more though I forgot
Just what it was and said,
But all the same that is a lot
To find in just one head.

Dragonfly
Georgia Heard

It skims the pond's surface,
searching for gnats, mosquitoes, and flies.
Outspread wings blur with speed.
It touches down
and stops to sun itself on the dock.
Wings flicker and still:
stained-glass windows
with sun shining through.

I write first drafts with only the good angel on my
shoulder, the voice that approves of everything I
write. This voice doesn't ask questions like, "Is this
good? Is this a poem? Are you a poet?" I keep that
voice at a distance, letting only the good angel whis-
per to me: "Trust yourself." You can't worry a poem
into existence. *—Georgia Heard*

Try This: Poem of Direct Address
A poem of direct address talks directly to another person or thing. The thing can be anything: plant, animal, mailbox, Godzilla, your sneakers, or, as in Richard Edwards's poem, a maggot:

To a Maggot in an Apple

You lie there like a baby,
Frail and soft and curled,
I'm sorry that I broke in
To your safe white world.
I really didn't mean to,
Just blame my appetite
For laying bare your cradle
And letting in the light.
One question then I'll leave you
To slumber in the bin—
I'm feeling rather queasy,
Er . . . did you have a twin?

A poem of direct address is a good way to take care of some unfinished business, or to say some things that you've been keeping to yourself. The reason for writing a poem to someone or something could be:

anger . . . at the alarm clock, a friend who betrayed your confidence, people who have no respect for the earth;

admiration . . . for the author who wrote your favorite book, a river (as Naomi Shihab Nye does in "Little Blanco River" on page 86), your mom for being a great single parent;

respect . . . for the teacher who's tough but fair, your friend who had to make a very tough decision, an athlete for her stand on drugs;

thanks . . . for your older brother for giving you a ride to the mall, your dog for keeping your feet warm in bed in January, your father for understanding what you're going through;

bewilderment . . . at a team that keeps on losing, at your armpits for starting to sweat when the new boy sits at your lunch table, at the sun for coming up so early every morning.

Not only can you write a direct address poem to people and things that are close to you, but you can also write a poem to something or somebody you've never met, like the person who invented pizza, the snow for canceling school the day your (unfinished!) science report was due, or the woman who plays the alto sax on your street corner. The only limit is your imagination.

Other direct address poems in this book are "Zebra" by Bobbi Katz (page 111) and "My Horse, Fly Like a Bird," a Lakota warrior's song adapted by Virginia Driving Hawk Sneve (page 46).

The Animals Are Leaving
Charles Webb

One by one, like guests at a late party,
they shake our hands and step into the dark:
Arabian ostrich; Tasmanian emu; Guadalupe
storm petrel; Long-eared kit fox; Mysterious starling.

One by one, like sheep counted to close our eyes,
they leap the fence and disappear into the woods:
Atlas bear; Passenger pigeon; North Island laughing owl;
Great auk; Dodo; Eastern wapiti; Badlands bighorn sheep.

One by one, like gradeschool friends, they move
away and fade out of our memory:
Portuguese ibex; Blue buck; Auroch; Oregon bison;
Spanish imperial eagle; Japanese wolf; Hawksbill
sea turtle; Cape lion; Heath hen; Raiatea thrush.

One by one, like school kids at a fire drill, they march outside,
and keep marching even when, through screams behind them
and the stench of smoke, they hear teachers cry "Come back!"
Waved albatross; White-bearded spider monkey; Pygmy

29

chimpanzee; Australian night parrot; Turquoise parakeet;
Cape York paradise parakeet; Indian cheetah; Korean tiger;
Eastern harbor seal; Ceylon elephant; Great Indian rhinoceros;
West African manatee; Pacific right whale; Humpback whale;
Fin whale; Blue whale . . .

One by one, like actors after a play that ran for years
and wowed the world, they link their hands and bow for us
once more before the curtain falls.

E E E E E E E E E E E E E E E

Don't worry about not measuring up to other writers.
No one has the same genetic makeup, the same life
experiences as you. No one else sees the world quite
the way you do, or can express it quite the same way.
You're already the world's foremost expert on you.

—Charles Webb

HARVEY
Judith Viorst

Harvey doesn't laugh about how I stay short while everybody
    grows.
Harvey remembers I like jellybeans—except black.
Harvey lends me shirts I don't have to give back.
I'm scared of ghosts and only Harvey knows.

Harvey thinks I will when I say someday I will marry Margie Rose.
Harvey shares his lemonade—sip for sip.
He whispers "zip" when I forget to zip.
He swears I don't have funny-looking toes.

Harvey calls me up when I'm in bed with a sore throat and runny
    nose.
Harvey says I'm nice—but not *too* nice.
And if there is a train to Paradise,
I won't get on it unless Harvey goes.

FOR YOU
Karla Kuskin

Here is a building
I have built for you.
The bricks are butter yellow.
Every window shines.
And at each an orange cat is curled,
lulled by the summer sun.
The door invites you in.
The mat is warm.
Inside there is a chair
so soft and blue
the pillows look like sky.
In all the world
no one but you
may sit in that cloud chair.
I'll sit near by.

Advice? How about: 1. If you do not like to write, try it, and 2. If you like to write, write more. I did not have sisters, brothers, or television when I was growing up. Making up stories and verses was a way to keep myself company. It still is. You can sing to yourself, have conversations with yourself on paper. Writing can be an adventure, it can be a comfort, it can help you figure out what you think and feel. You can write yourself through a problem or out of a bad mood or you can write for the pure pleasure of putting words together in your very own particular way.

—Karla Kuskin

Frog
Jim Harrison

First memory
of swimming underwater:
eggs of frogs hanging in diaphanous clumps
from green lily pad stems;
at night in the tent I heard
the father of it all booming
and croaking in the reeds.

Chinatown Games
Wing Tek Lum

1. Choosing Sides

Little girls
on the sidewalk
chanting in a circle
an even number of them
each offering
a hand outstretched
some palms up
some down.
When by chance
an equal number
show up as down
they gather their teams
ready to play
no hint of ability
just the fun of the game.

2. Sugar Stuck Beans

An even number of kids:
one of them It.
Safety is found
in sticking together—
a pair of beans.
The It can tag you
only if you're alone.
The little ones scream
weave about parked cars
arms locked.
Some sacrifice security
gladly breaking a pair
to distract the It
saving another
dodging all by himself.

3. Hawk Grabbing Chicks

Arms waving
the mother hen
holds her ground
in front of the hawk
her children undulating
in a single line
behind her.

The hawk must go around
to snatch any stray
who might let go
as the hen angles
towards the hydrant
her noisy brood
hands to waist clinging on
for dear life.

Kick the Can
Robert Wallace

In the long after-suppers of summer
kids playing kick-the-can, like tiny
ghosts running here and there among
the trees, across the lawns, hold off

the weight of darkness. And the lights
go on in houses; radios tell
the weather, Doolittle over Tokyo,
or Robert Kennedy in L.A.

Hidden too well, deep in the barberry
by widower McCann's white porch,
or in the tomato-patches in yards
beyond the unlit alley, I hear

the can go clunking down the walk
and "One-two-three" and "All-in-free."
The years go by. I am not caught,
nor called home, all the long dark long.

Yellow Glove
Naomi Shihab Nye

What can a yellow glove mean in a world of motorcars and governments?

I was small, like everyone. Life was a string of precautions:
Don't kiss the squirrel before you bury him, don't suck candy,
pop balloons, drop watermelons, watch T.V. When the new
gloves appeared one Christmas, tucked in soft tissue. I hear it
trailing me: Don't lose the yellow gloves.

G G G G G G G G G G G G G

I was small, there was too much to remember. One day, waving at a stream–the ice had cracked, winter chipping down, soon we would sail boats and roll into ditches–I let a glove go. Into the stream, sucked under the street. Since when did streets have mouths? I walked home on a desperate road. Gloves cost money. We didn't have much. I would tell no one. I would wear the yellow glove that was left and keep the other hand in a pocket. I knew my mother's eyes had tears they had not cried yet and I didn't want to be the one to make them flow. It was the prayer I spoke secretly, folding socks, lining up donkeys in windowsills. I would be good, a promise made to the roaches who scouted my closet at night. If you don't get in my bed, I will be good. And they listened. I had a lot to fulfill.

The months rolled down like towels out of a machine. I sang and drew and fattened the cat. Don't scream, don't lie, don't cheat, don't fight–you could hear it anywhere. A pebble could show you how to be smooth, tell the truth. A field could show how to sleep without walls. A stream could remember how to drift and change–the next June I was stirring the stream like a soup, telling my brother dinner would be ready if he'd only hurry up with the bread, when I saw it. The yellow glove draped on a twig. A reckless survivor. A muddy flag.

Where had it been in the three gone months? I could wash it, fold it in my winter drawer with its sister, no one in that world would ever know. There were miracles on Harvey Street. Children walked home in yellow light. Trees were reborn and gloves traveled far, but returned. A thousand miles later, what can a yellow glove mean in a world of bankbooks and stereos?

Part of the difference between floating and going down.

Returning the Red Gloves
Siv Cedering

I am returning
the red
gloves
you left in Vera's
pocket

They are soft shells
that miss
the snails that would give them
their own slow
speed

They are five-room houses
waiting for their inhabitants
to come home

They are red wings
that have forgotten
how to fly

When you receive them
put them on

41

for like lovers who warm each other
all night
you will warm them
and they will warm
your hands

which must be
lost
Valentines
without
their envelopes

H H H H H H H H H H **H**

Try This: How-to Poem

If you've ever tried putting something together from a set of directions—maybe assembling your brother's bike or hooking up your new stereo—you know how important it is that the directions be clear. Writing a good how-to poem is a lot like writing good directions. You need to find the right words and use them in the best order. And you need to use just the number of words necessary to say what you need to say. See what Ralph Fletcher did in "How to Make a Snow Angel":

> Go alone or with a best friend.
> Find a patch of unbroken snow.
>
> Walk on tiptoes. Step backwards
> Into your very last footprints.
>
> Slowly sit back onto the snow.
> Absolutely do not use your hands.
>
> By now you should be lying flat
> With snow fitting snug around you.

H H H H H H H H H H H H

Let your eyes drink some blue sky.
Close them. Breathe normally.

Move your arms back and forth.
Concentrate. Think: snow angel.

In a minute don't be surprised
If you start feeling a little funny.

Both big and small. Warm and cold.
Your breath light as a snowflake.

Sweep your legs back and forth
But keep both eyes tightly closed.

Keep moving the arms until they
Lift, tremble, wobble or float.

Stand without using your hands.
Take time to get your balance.

Take three deep breaths.
Open your eyes.

Stretch. Float. Fly!

When you write a how-to poem, pick something that's fairly simple. "How to Write a Term Paper" might not be a good topic. Try something like "How to Make the Perfect Sandwich" or "How to Catch Her Attention without Getting Caught by the Teacher."

You might begin your poem with "First, . . ." That will give you the chance to use good connecting words like *second, third, next, finally.* Don't be afraid to use your imagination with your instructions. You might start off with sensible instructions, but that doesn't mean that you can't work in a few inventive ideas or build to zanier ideas as your poem goes on. Once you've written your first draft, read through it and cross out all the unnecessary words. Remember, you are writing directions (and a poem), so you want to include only the best words.

Another type of how-to poem is one in which you suggest ways that somebody can be something else. For example, you might write "Ways to Be a Summer Day" or "Learn to Be a Cloud." These are like list poems, but they are more "how-to" in nature. This type of poem is a good way to imagine what it might feel like to be a thing, like rain, a subway, or a broken heart.

If you want to write poetry, you must have poems that deeply move you. Poems you can't live without. I think of a poem as the blood in a blood transfusion, given from the heart of the poet to the heart of the reader. Seek after poems that live inside you, poems that move through your veins.   —Ralph Fletcher

My Horse, Fly Like a Bird
Virginia Driving Hawk Sneve

My horse, fly like a bird
To carry me far
From the arrows of my enemies,
And I will tie red ribbons
To your streaming hair.

(adapted from a Lakota warrior's song to his horse)

H H H H H H H H H H H H H

Which
William Stafford

Which of the horses
we passed yesterday whinnied
all night in my dreams?
    I want that one.

Where Do My Pages Come From? Many writers, I think, try to write good poems, but my pages just come to me, mostly in early morning. They drift into their form out of tangles in my life. They find their way to become whatever they are:—parts of some unrealized story. —William Stafford

---

Try This: Haiku

Haiku, an ancient Japanese poetic form, captures in a few words the essence of a season and a scene. Each haiku is seventeen syllables long, divided into three lines of five, seven, and five syllables. Traditional haiku almost always contain some sort of seasonal word or phrase and usually are like a snapshot—a picture of a small scene—rather than a movie—something sweeping that switches scenes and may tell many stories. One last haiku rule: They describe in the present tense. Here's a haiku written by J. W. Hackett:

> A bitter morning:
> sparrows sitting together
> without any necks

To write a haiku, start by taking a look out your window. Which window? Any window: your clubhouse, classroom, school bus, grandmother's apartment, the grocery store, church. Which window you look from isn't as important as how carefully you look. You need to really *see* things. It's a good idea to have your writing journal handy when you do look. That way you can write down what you see. Don't worry about writing a haiku while you're looking. That may affect what you see. Instead just look and write down the details. If you see a blue jay, write that down. Don't write just "bird." Notice details to use in your haiku.

After you've looked and taken notes, read over what you've seen and start thinking about how you can capture one scene. Remember, you're trying to "write a snapshot" so you want to focus on the small details. Since you can only use seventeen syllables in your haiku, it's crucial that you find the best words to describe your scene. Don't use three words when two or one will do. If you have trouble finding the right word, check out your thesaurus. It may have the word you're looking for.

Once you write out your poem, you'll need to look for things that can be condensed or cut out. Your poem should have seventeen syllables and the three lines should break at natural-sounding places. You can indent each line of your poem or start each line at the left margin.

After you've written some haiku that capture the different seasons, you might want to try a different kind of poem that *looks* like a haiku but sounds quite different. You could call these Kooku, since they work with zany subjects. Here are two examples to show you what I mean:

> Baby sister nags
>> she never goes anyplace . . .
>>> I'd love to send her.

> O, cinnamon bun,
>> I am ready to eat you . . .
>>> Then raisin takes wing!

I think you can see these are haiku . . . with a twist! Have fun when you write your own.

INVITATION
Bobbi Katz

Come into my so snug house.
Be like me,
a hollow thing
ready for rhythms.
Listen.
Listen to the rain
strum-drumming on the rooftop
softer
louder
LOUDER
then whispering
returning
insisting
persisting.
Listen.
Listen to the wind
rattling bare, black branches
then whipping them
faster and faster
slowly releasing them

only to return.
Is that a car or a truck
swaggering through the flooded streets?
Don't look.
Let your ears answer.
Come.
Hear the water
rushing down the rooftop gutters,
gushing into a well of pebbles.
Be like me
a hollow thing
ready for rhythms,
listening,
listening.
Come into my so snug house.

I know a poem is finished when I can't find another word to cut. My favorite poems are like vitamins. They are capsules of feelings, pictures, sounds. Rhythmic combinations of words that give new energy to language. Warning: Rhyme is fun, but it can get bossy! Use it to say what *you* want to say. Don't let it take over your ideas!　　　　—Bobbi Katz

J J J J J J J J J J J J J J
J

In a Jewelry Store

Mary Ann Coleman

The hands of watches drop intervals
like the beginning of rain
or a quilt's continuous pattern.
Rings flash light.

After Grandmother sailed
the sun-riffled water
from Germany
shielding her eyes
from the sudden glare
of America,
it was gold like this
that drew her
through the Ohio River Valley
to fix her husband's stern face
in our family album.
His hands gripped
the shining of nails
he pounded into shoes.
Pale shadows of children

J J J J J J J J J J J J J J J J J

earned the fruit that lay
next to Grandmother's cumulous dumplings
and pot roasts glistening with streams of oil.

Portsmouth, Ohio. Mouth-of-the-port.
Years the river rose, pushing over boundaries
they'd declared enough, claiming whole clapboard houses.
The Ohio, shrugging off dresses and shirts
that slid over riverbanks and blistered on mud-caked trees.
The man, shoveling, bent to his long work,
swearing in German.

I travel through them,
a shoemaker's grandchild,
standing before rows
of diamonds and bright metal,
remembering Grandmother, her hair
pulled tight in a knot. How she told
of her time on the flood plain,
sweeping the dried mud out,
her mind's single image
pansies in immaculate window boxes
leaning toward the gold
coin of the sun.

♩ ♩ ♩ ♩ ♩ ♩ ♩ ♩ ♩ ♩ ♩ ♩ ♩ ♩ ♩ ♩

Cow
Marilyn Singer

I approve of June
Fresh food to chew
   and chew
   and chew
Lots of room to move around
   or lie down
Not too hot
Not too cold
Not too wet
Not too dry
A good roof of sky over me and my calf
Who's now halfway up
   on new legs
He'll want a meal real soon
Yes, I approve of June

♪ ♪ ♪ ♪ ♪ ♪ ♪ ♪ ♪ ♪ ♪ ♪ ♪ ♪ ♪ ♪ ♪

The famous poet Samuel Taylor Coleridge said that poetry is the best words in the best order. I try to follow that advice. If the words I use don't sound like the best ones, I try others until I find the words that do. The same goes for their order. I arrange and rearrange phrases until they sound just right.

Order has a lot to do with sound and rhythm. I read each of my poems aloud to myself and ask, does it sing? I don't mean the way a song does. A friend of mine said that a poem has a different music than a song, and I agree with him. I listen for that music.

—Marilyn Singer

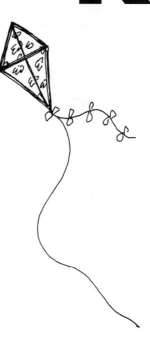

kɪᴛᴇ
Valerie Worth

The kite, kept
Indoors, wears
Dead paper
On tight-
Boned wood,
Pulls at the tied
Cord only
By its weight—

But held
To the wind,
It is another thing,
Turned strong,
Struck alive,
Wild to be torn
Away from the hand
Into high air:

Where it rides
Alone,

K K K K K K K K K K K K

Glad,
A small, clear
Wing, having
Nothing at all
To do
With string.

The Kite That Braved Old Orchard Beach

X. J. Kennedy

The kite that braved Old Orchard Beach
    But fell and snapped its spine
Hangs in our attic out of reach
    All tangled in its twine.

My father says, "Let's throw it out,"
    But I won't let him. No,
There has to be some quiet spot
    Where cracked-up heroes go.

Try This: Letter Poem

One of the good things about a poem is that often it is short enough to easily share with a friend. The most obvious way to share such verse is by writing it in the form of a letter. It's important to remember that even though you intend your poem to be a letter, it still must be the best poem you can write.

You might want to share your feelings with your friend, as Lilian Moore does in "Letter to a Friend":

> Come soon.
>
> Everything is lusting
> for light,
> thrusting
> up
> up
> splitting the earth,
> opening flaring fading,
> seed
> into shoot
> bud
> into flower,
> nothing
> beyond its hour.

Come soon.

The apple bloom has melted
like
spring snow.

The lilac
changed the air,
surprising
every breath.

Low in the field
wild strawberries
fatten.

Come soon.

It's a matter of
life.

And death.

Perhaps you want to set the record straight, or perhaps your poem is really an apology for something
you did. Of course, a poem could be a great way to
write a thank-you note. If you do write a letter poem
to a friend or relative, think about giving it or mailing
it to that person. True, sometimes it's risky to share

your feelings, but the results can be rewarding. You might begin to iron out a difference of opinion, or you might find that the person you are writing to has feelings similar to yours.

You can also write a letter as a historical figure or a person from literature. What would George Washington say, for instance, in a letter to a friend about the time he chopped down his father's cherry tree? Or what if a bank teller wrote of the time her bank was robbed by Jesse James and his gang? Can you imagine Dr. Watson writing a letter to his sister telling about his adventures with his friend Sherlock Holmes? If you think of important historical figures and characters from literature, I bet you could come up with lots of ideas for letters that these people could "write" in your poems.

Of course, you can write a poem as a letter from an imaginary person, too. Let your imagination run wild and come up with some great characters who might write interesting, funny, or sad letters. What would the bearded lady say to her husband? What about the cop who works the beat in a dangerous neighborhood? Or the woman who works in the art museum, making sure that no one touches the paintings? If you use your imagination, these people can "write" great letters.

Try This: List Poem

We've all made lists. Maybe a list of books we wanted to check out from the library. Or a list of people to send party invitations. A list is a good way to organize things, a way to bring order. Any good poem has its own order, but this is especially true of a list poem.

A list poem is not merely a list of words or phrases as they drift from your brain down your neck and arm to your hand, which writes them in your notebook. That's the way a list poem will *start*, but if it's a good poem, you will make sure that you have some reason for listing things the way you do. Bobbi Katz imagined herself to be the rain and wrote her list poem "Things to Do If You Are the Rain":

> Be gentle.
> Hide the edges of buildings.
> Plip, plop in puddles.
> Tap, tap, tap against the rooftops.
> Sing your very own song!
> Make the grass green.
> Make the world smell special.
> Race away on a gray cloud.
> Sign your name with a rainbow.

A list poem can be serious or humorous. You could, for instance, write "Things I Wish I Said to My Friend

L L L L L L L L L L L L L

Before She Moved Away." Or you can write "Things to Say to Break a Date." The lines in these poems might be longer lines made up of phrases and sentences. On the other hand, your poem might be made up of very short lines if you were going to write "Things That Squeak" or "Quiet Things" or "Morning Sounds Outside My Window."

I'm sure you can think up other ideas for your list poem, but let me suggest a few:

Things I just can't believe!
Things to do while waiting for
 my brother/ sister to get off the phone
 my friend to call
 my teacher to call on me for the homework I
  didn't quite finish
Things I'll always keep
Things I should have done
Things that . . . buzz, snarl, clank, click
Things that are . . . green, sad, silly, too beautiful for
 words

After you have your first list, take a good look at it. Your list poem is likely lurking in those words. Can you see something that the items have in common? That may be one way to organize your poem. Another way may be chronological order. For example, if you're writing a poem about morning sounds, you might begin with the sound that wakes you up and end with the sound that you hear before you finally get out of bed. Look for some unusual connection, something a reader might not think of right away. Remember that you want your poem to be interesting not just for you, but for anyone else who might read it. Maybe one poem will include only concrete things you can touch or see, but another poem might be better if you mix the concrete with intangibles.

As you work on your poem, read it out loud. What does it sound like? Can you hear a rhythm? If you change a couple of words or lines, will that make the poem sound better?

Speaking of sound, list poems normally don't rhyme, but that doesn't mean you can't rhyme yours. Richard Edwards rhymed his list poem "Useless Things" (page 102).

A Lesson in Manners
John Ciardi

Someone told me someone said
You should never be bad till you've been fed.
You may, you know, be sent to bed
Without your supper.—And there you are
With nothing to eat. Not even a jar
Of pickle juice, nor a candy bar.
No, nothing to eat and nothing to drink,
And all night long to lie there and think
About washing baby's ears with ink,
Or nailing the door shut, or sassing Dad,
Or about whatever you did that was bad,
And wishing you hadn't, and feeling sad.

Now then, if what I'm told is true,
What I want to say to you—and you—
Is: MIND YOUR MANNERS. They just
          won't do.
If you have to be bad, you must learn to wait
Till after supper. Be good until eight.
If you let your badness come out late

It doesn't hurt to be sent to bed.
Well, not so much. So use your head:
Don't be bad till you've been fed.

Try This: Memory Poem

Memory is one of your most important assets. It helps you store all sorts of information and experiences. You can remember facts, like your father's birthday, your mother's phone number at work, the batting average of your favorite baseball player, and the color of the house you used to live in. But you can also remember experiences, like when your baby sister came

66

home for the first time, the day your grandfather died, getting your first pet, and playing your best Halloween prank. Ellen Gilchrist recalls her memories with humor in "The Best Meal I Ever Had Anywhere":

> At the wonderful table of my grandfather
> Bunky got the high chair
> Dooley got the Webster's Unabridged Dictionary
> and I got the Compton's Pictured Encyclopedia
> Volumes A, B, D, and E.
> The best meal I ever had anywhere
> was one Sunday Pierce Noblin
> wired the salt shaker to a dry cell battery
> Dolly got a fishbone caught in her throat
> and almost died
> Sudie went into the parlor to sulk
> and when no one was looking
> I stabbed Bunky in the knee
> with Onnie Maud's pearl handled wedding fork.

Some of your best poems will come from your memories. If you think that you don't have a very good memory, don't worry. Work with what you do remember and make up the rest. The important thing is writing a good poem, so if you wish to make up or change some details, that's perfectly all right. You're trying to write a poem, not history. That's one of the great things about writing poetry: You don't have to stick to the facts.

Many of our memories are connected with things, so if you have trouble thinking of something to write about, look through that box or drawer where you keep your treasures. That movie ticket stub, scuffed and scarred yo-yo, or fake pearl necklace may help you recall an experience that was very important to you. It may be a pleasant memory, but be prepared for some unhappy memories, because some of our strongest memories may be sad ones. Even if your memories are sad, try to write about them. That may help you understand them better.

If you keep a writer's journal, that's the perfect place to write down things that remind you of other things. Smells, for example, often trigger memories. Maybe the smell of the school cafeteria brings back a memory. Or the smell of your father's after-shave lotion reminds you of the times he read picture books to you when you were a baby. Tastes and sounds might also bring back some memories. Write them down in your journal. Then, when you want something to write about, you'll have some ideas.

Other journal lists that might help you are:

heroes: Who are your heroes at this point in your life? Can you remember people who used to be your heroes? They may include people in sports or movies or your family.

games: What games do you like to play? Board games, street games, computer games? What games did you play when you were younger? Do you associate those games with certain friends? Can you think of a particularly memorable game?

friends: Whom do you consider your best friend? Do you have a group of people you consider your best friends? Can you think of any of your friends from years ago? Recall some memorable things you did with some of your friends.

Another trick you can try is to write "I remember the time . . ." or "I remember when . . ." at the top of a journal page. Look at the words, then close your eyes and let your mind see what it will recall. When your memory starts supplying details, open your eyes and write them down. You might be surprised at what you can remember!

Details are important in any good writing, but especially in poetry of memory. As a poet, you want to recreate a scene so your reader can be there. So when you are writing a memory poem, make sure you use details that appeal to our senses: sight, sound, smell, taste, and touch. You won't include every sense in every poem, of course, but make an effort to include those details that create a vivid picture for your reader. Don't be satisfied saying, "It was cold" when you could say, "My fingers were like icicles."

You can create a clear picture by using comparisons. One kind of comparison is a simile, which is a comparison using *like* or *as*. You might say something like, "His voice sounded like a knife running across a slice of burnt toast." Another type of comparison is a metaphor, when you more directly compare two things. For example: "My fingers were icicles." A good comparison can go a long way in helping your reader see and feel what you're writing about.

Mark Twain said that the difference between the right word and the almost-right word was like the difference between lightning and a lightning bug. Make sure you're not satisfied until you've found the right word.

M M M M M M M M M M M

Corn-growing Music
Leo Dangel

In that hazy stillness
between summer and fall,
they say you can hear
corn grow. Leaves stir
and sing a whispering song.

I look over my field
and want to conduct
my million-stalk chorus.
I could wave my arms
like a lunatic—louder,
louder, you bastards,
I still owe the bank
for your seed.

I listen again as leaves
flutter down the rows.
Maybe each stalk sings
its own growing song,
as I sing mine, or maybe
it's only the wind.

The Night
Myra Cohn Livingston

The night
    creeps in
    around my head
    and snuggles down
    upon the bed,
    and makes lace pictures
    on the wall
    but doesn't say a word at all.

Nothing takes the place of keeping a journal, in which to record observations and thoughts, a phrase, a word, an idea that can be used when there is leisure to write, nor is there any substitute for observation: the time taken to carefully examine and respond to the world around us.　　—Myra Cohn Livingston

---

NOSE
Steven Kroll

I chose
A nose
From the pile
In the aisle.

With luck
It stuck
Adding style
To my smile.

As a writer, don't overlook anything that comes your way, whether it's within your own experience or from the farthest reaches of your imagination. The best ideas for poems or stories can come from the most unexpected places. —Steven Kroll

Try This: Opposites

I discovered opposites when I read *Opposites* by Richard Wilbur. The book is filled with short, rhyming poems. I read the book again and thought that young writers would enjoy writing opposites. I was right! Read these examples written by some of my writing students:

> What is the opposite of kind?
> A goat that butts you from behind.
>
> The opposite of a chair
> Is sitting down with nothing there.
>
> What is the opposite of school?
> It would be something very cool.
> Because school is something I hate,
> The opposite must be great.

An opposite is made up of pairs of lines that rhyme, and it can be two, four, six, or eight lines long or longer if you can think up enough things that are the opposite of your subject. An opposite will frequently begin with the question "What is the opposite of . . . ?" If you choose to begin your poem with that question, the rest of the poem should answer that question. The most important thing about an opposite is that it really *is* about things that are the opposite of your subject.

When you're trying to think of a subject for your first poem, it might be helpful to think of an adjective, because it will probably be easier to think of things that are the opposite of that adjective. For example, it's easy to think of things that are the opposite of tall, round, or huge. So you might begin with "What is the opposite of loud?" Next, you need to think up specific things that are the opposite of loud and try to find rhymes at the same time. For example:

> What is the opposite of loud?
> The noise made by a passing cloud,
> A whisper in the dead of night
> An owl waiting in moonlight

When you write an opposite, it's important to know when the poem is complete. Sometimes you may write a two-line opposite and have the feeling that you can say more about the subject. At other times, a two-line opposite will say all you want.

o o o o o o o o o o o o o o o

Peeling an Orange
Eve Merriam

Tearing the skin carelessly
like yesterday's newspaper

or meticulously,
a carpenter restoring the spiral staircase in the castle

the juice
a rainspout gurgle

the smell
invading the fog.

October Talk
J. Patrick Lewis

Says the cornstalk
    ears
    can hear
    whispertalk

o o o o o o o o o o o o o o

Say the shadows
        leap
        surprise

Sighs the night wind
        wish I wish

Says a Mother
        to a witchy-girl
        ride

Says the wolf-boy
        knocking
        grrr

Says my cat
        black on the new moon
        oh

Shouts the house on the hill
        come round
        all around

Sings the barn owl
        home

○ ○ ○ ○ ○ ○ ○ ○ ○ ○ ○ ○ ○ ○

A couple of centuries ago, the English wit Samuel
Johnson offered this terrific piece of advice. It's especially useful, I think, for young writers and poets:
Never trust people, Johnson said, who write more
than they read.   —J. Patrick Lewis

porches
Valerie Worth

On the front porch
Chairs sit still;

The table will receive
Summer drinks;

They wait, arranged,
Strange and polite.

On the back porch
Garden tools spill;

An empty basket
Leans to one side;

The watering can
Rusts among friends.

One good way to start writing poetry is to *read* all kinds of poetry: not just in order to imitate it (though this can sometimes be a useful exercise) but to fill up your head with it, to absorb it, to make poetry an essential part of how you view the world.

—Valerie Worth

Prayer for Fish
Ronald Wallace

Twenty below. It is too cold
to talk. Words break in the air.
The tips of my fingers crack and split.
My ice auger and skimmer,
my waxworms and fish bucket
huddle beside me. The wind
clips its swivel to my face.

P P P P P P P P P P P P P

The fish aren't biting.
I imagine them huddled
around my cold bait, moving slow.
It will take them all day.
I wait with the other ice fishermen,
bent over our holes as in prayer:

Let the fish leave their sleep
and rise up our poles;
let our fingers recover
their delicate grace;
let the patience of walleye and pike
remind us:
all cold things will melt,
all sleeping things wake,
keeping their proper seasons.

Don't quit. One of the most difficult qualities you must develop as a writer is the discipline to keep going, even if what you're writing seems terrible. Some of my best poems almost didn't get written because the first few lines (or the whole first draft!) seemed stupid or boring.   —Ronald Wallace

Try This: Persona Poem

If you've ever had fun dressing up for Halloween or a costume party, or if you've played a part in a school or church play, you have some idea what it's like to write a persona poem. Writing a persona poem is like wearing a mask. You *become* some other person or some other thing, and you write about what that's like. That's what Marilyn Singer did in "Timber Rattlesnake":

> Summer it still is
> > Yes
> September stones
> Warm bones
> Warm blood
> Strike I still can
> > Yes
> Snare and swallow the harvesting mouse
> > > the shuffling rat
> But slant they do the sun's rays
> Shorter grow the days
> > Yes
> Soon September stones
> Chill bones
> Chill blood
> Stiff shall I grow

P P P P P P P P P P P P P

And so below I'll slide
Beneath stones
Beneath soil
Coil I still can
      Yes
Sleep safe
Sleep sound
Snake underground

The great thing about writing a persona poem is that you can "be" whatever or whomever you'd like to be. Just let your imagination go! You can be a vegetable or an animal. "Timber Rattlesnake," for example, is told from a snake's point of view. How would you feel if you were a potato growing up underground or a hippopotamus lumbering to the watering hole? If you want to warn people about endangered species, maybe you can write a poem as an animal that is in danger of becoming extinct. Or if you like to hang out with a gang, maybe you can write about being a wolf.

It's important that you imagine being the thing or animal you are writing about. How did you come about? What has your life been like? What are some of the things you like or dislike? Do you make any sounds?

Writing a persona poem is a good way to express

some feelings that might be difficult for you to put into words. For example, if you feel you're too tall and thin, you might write a poem about what it feels like being a giraffe. If you feel left out much of the time, you might write about what it's like being the last peach in the fruit bowl when all the others have been chosen for a fruit salad.

If writing as a vegetable or an animal doesn't interest you, perhaps you want to write a persona poem as an elderly person or a baby. Another idea is to be a character from a nursery rhyme or fairy tale. What would it be like to be Mary's "little lamb" or Cinderella's mean stepmother or one of the kids of the "old woman who lived in a shoe"?

Need more ideas? How about writing a persona poem as a person with an unusual occupation, like the person who gets shot out of a cannon, a skyscraper window washer, or the person who runs the scoreboard at a baseball stadium? Or you could write a poem as a performer in a circus, a circus animal, or one of the vendors.

Once you've written a couple of persona poems that please you, try writing a dialogue poem in which two people, animals, or things talk to each other. For example, what would a conversation between bread and butter sound like? You might want to write a dialogue poem in which a couple of your teachers or your parents talk about you.

The Question
Dennis Lee

1

If I could teach you how to fly
Or bake an elderberry pie
Or turn the sidewalk into stars
Or play new songs on an old guitar
Or if I knew the way to heaven,
The names of night, the taste of seven
And owned them all, to keep or lend—
Would you come and be my friend?

2

You cannot teach me how to fly.
I love the berries but not the pie.
The sidewalks are for walking on,
And an old guitar has just one song.
The names of night cannot be known,
The way to heaven cannot be shown.
You cannot keep, you cannot lend—
But still I want you for my friend.

?

R R R R R R R R R R R

Little Blanco River
Naomi Shihab Nye

You're only a foot deep

Under green water
your smooth shale skull
is slick and cool

Blue drangonfly
skims you like a stone

skipping
skipping
it never goes under

You square-dance with boulders
make a clean swiching sound
centuries of skirts
lifting and falling
in delicate rounds

No one makes a state park out of you
You're not deep enough

Little Blanco River
Don't ever get too big

Write luxuriously, abundantly, fill whole pages, making little notes to yourself in the margins. Don't worry about "saying it perfectly in a condensed way." Don't ask yourself after every line, "Is this right?" These things will only paralyze you. Write generously, knowing you can shape and trim later.

—Naomi Shihab Nye

Rainspout
John Updike

Up the house's nether corner,
Snaky-skilled, the burglar shinnies,
Peeking, cautious, in the dormer,
Creeping, wary, where the tin is.

Stealthily he starts to burgle.
Hear his underhanded mutter;

R R R R R R R R R R R R R R

Hear him, with a guilty gurgle,
Pour his loot into the gutter.

My suggestion to young poets is to learn to rhyme and scan, by reading poems that rhyme and scan. Poetry without even a ghost of formal metrics is just a jumble of words dumped on the page.   —John Updike

Try This: Shape Poem

"Throwing My Weight" is a shape poem. Some people call it a concrete poem. In a shape poem, the arrangement of the letters and words on the page adds meaning to the poem. In Monica Kulling's poem, the arrangement of the words imitates the movement of a discus thrower as she spins and releases the discus.

I take the cold, flat disk turn circles with my feet around and round and then I let it fly—a silver sailing bird!

If you'd like to try your hand at a shape poem, you need to come up with a shape that isn't too complicated. A house, car, or flowerpot might work for you. Or try a swimming pool, park bench, or bus. Draw that shape. Make sure it's large enough for you to fit the words of your poem on it. Next, write down whatever you can about your subject: what it looks like, how it sounds, what it does, and so on. Remember to be specific. Once you're satisfied with your list, pick out the best things. Maybe you'll pick visual images, or perhaps sounds the object makes. You might choose a number of things that give a full picture of your object. Finally, you need to fit your words into your shape. You can write your words along the edges of your shape, or you can fill in the entire shape with the words. Which way works best for you and your shape? For another example, read "Snake Date" by Jean Balderston (page 94).

Sparklers
Joan LaBombard

Nothing's more marvelous than sparklers!
Not pinwheels or Roman Candles,
or the boom of a Cherry Bomb.
Not the Snakes like horror-film worms
writhing out of a pill.
Not even the Fountain of Pearls.
There's nothing so magical when you're nine
as to write your name on the dark
with a fiery wand
while the afterimage hangs there
telling you who you are—
to light star after star from the one dying
till you are your own firefly.

When "inspiration" comes, the best way to be ready is to have spent many hours, years even, working on less-than-inspired poems. Then the lucky moment arrives, and the craft you have practiced so patiently will flow into place supporting and carrying your poem to its finest possible fulfillment.   —Joan LaBombard

---

LINE STORM

for Gene Frumkin

Mark Vinz

Only the wind is moving now, the grass
        turning upon itself.
The farmer's boots stand empty on the porch.
Even the windows sleep.

Suddenly the eyes of the clouds are open,
the lightning stalks the windrows five miles down,
        closer and closer . . .

Out in the fields, all the
abandoned machines begin to awaken—
cornpickers, combines, balers
circling in a heavy dance,
rooting the ground with their snouts.
An ancient John Deere tractor is leading them . . .
westward, toward the conspiracy of clouds,
        the iron voices of the lightning.

And now they are waiting:
steaming and shuddering in the first assault of rain.

S S S S S S S S S S S S S S S

Some of the most astonishing discoveries about the writing process are also the simplest—such as the changes that can come about from writing at different times of the day and in different places. Too often our schedules put us into ruts of mood and habit.

                                              —Mark Vinz

SNAKE DATE
Jean Balderston

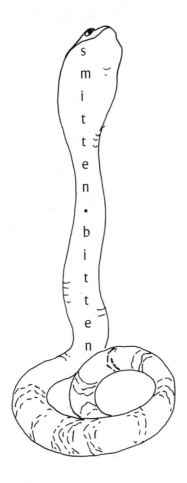

s
m
i
t
t
e
n
·
b
i
t
t
e
n

T T T T T T T T T T T **T**

On Susan's Toes
Paul Ruffin

By the pond in the park today I saw
your toes for the first time. You
had slipped off your sandals,
a Spring thing to do, yes, yes.
You were sitting on a tree root,
your feet together, your ten toes
in a line like pink children in church:
the older boys head to head, then
tapering to the babies at the ends.
They were startlingly well behaved.
Oh, one lifted her head, the tall one
beside big brother on the right,
but she was simply watching a bird.
I could not stop to stare, walked
on around the pond. Started back,
but you'd already packed them up
for the trip home, five to a carriage,
side by side. I had no chance to wave.
So, for today, goodbye to you, Susan
Mayne, and all your lovely children.

T T T T T T T T T T T T T

In choosing my subject matter, I always look for the sense of mystery in the most ordinary of experience: teaching my daughter about death and gravity, describing a boy's descent into a well to clean it out, recalling my grandmother's conversation with a couple of "Bible-thumpers."

As far as *writing* the poem goes, I stress the importance of powerful introductions and conclusions—without which the poem will probably fail—and the necessity of sense-assaulting imagery, without which the poem will fail *utterly.* —Paul Ruffin

T T T T T T T T T T T T T

Tugboat at Daybreak
Lillian Morrison

The necklace of the bridge
is already dimmed for morning
but a tug in a tiara
glides slowly up the river,
a jewel of the dawn,
still festooned in light.

The river seems to slumber
quiet in its bed,
as silently the tugboat,
a ghostlike apparition,
moves twinkling up the river
and disappears from sight.

Read good poetry—aloud.

Express *your* thoughts and feelings, not what you think you *should* feel.

Enjoy words—their sounds, meanings, and rhythms when strung together.

Notice things—their look, feel, taste, sound, smell, what they remind you of.

Care what and how you write but have fun doing it.   —Lillian Morrison

---

T T T T T T T T T T T T T

Try This: Takeoff

Sometimes when poets want to have fun, they take a poem that somebody else has written and imitate its style but write new words. In *Knock at a Star* X. J. Kennedy and Dorothy Kennedy called such a poem a "takeoff." *Mad* magazine has featured takeoffs for years in its "For Better or Verse" section. You may have done the same thing with your friends, or maybe at camp when you sang an old song but added new words that you made up. When I tried to do that with an old nursery rhyme, I had a wonderful time.

I used "Ten Little Indians" for my poem. But, since I wanted my poem to be very up-to-date, I wrote about visitors from outer space and called my poem "Ten Little Aliens":

Ten little aliens landed feeling fine
One bought a hot tub and then there were nine

Nine little aliens stayed up very late
One overslept and then there were eight.

Eight little aliens took the name of Kevin
One died laughing and then there were seven.

T T T T T T T T T T T T T

Seven little aliens studied magic tricks
One disappeared and then there were six.

Six little aliens learned how to drive
One missed the exit and then there were five.

Five little aliens polished the floor
One slipped and fell and then there were four.

Four little aliens climbed a tall tree
One lost his grip and then there were three.

Three little aliens visited the zoo
One liked the ape and then there were two.

Two little aliens baked in the sun
One got well-done and then there was one.

One little alien went looking for fun
He never came back and now there are none.

T T T T T T T T T T T T

Do you think you'd like to write a poem like this one? Of course, you don't have to write about aliens. Almost anything will do. Young writers I've worked with have written poems about slugs, brothers, and teachers, to name just a few subjects. And you don't need to start with ten. Any number will work. One writer I worked with asked if he could begin with one and work up to ten. I told him I wasn't sure that would work. He soon proved me wrong!

This is another poem that works with couplets. You'll notice that the first word of every couplet in "Ten Little Aliens" is a number. So is the last word. And the first word of each second line, except in the final couplet, is "one."

When you are ready to try your own takeoff, try to recall some nursery rhymes that you have read. You may remember rhymes like "Mary Had a Little Lamb," "There Was an Old Woman Who Lived in a Shoe," and "Jack and Jill." If you have a hard time remembering or if you want new ideas, grab one of your little brother's nursery rhyme books and thumb through it. I'm sure you'll find lots of rhymes that you can use.

THE LAST TYRANNOSAUR
Charles Webb

It's been winter for five years now.
The tv says the temperature has dropped
ten more degrees in the last hour.

I walk outside to feel it for myself.
My neighbor's stereo is blaring
"Gimme Shelter." Razor-toothed,

dragging his thick lizard tail,
he lumbers out, not seeing me,
and stares sadly up into the ceaseless snow.

101

Useless Things
Richard Edwards

A spout without a hole
A Swiss without a roll
Ladders without rungs
Taste without tongues,

A shepherd without sheep
A horn without a beep
Hockey without sticks
Candles without wicks,

Bzzzz

A pier without the sea
A buzz without a bee
A lid without a box
Keys without locks,

A harp without a string
A pong without a ping
A broom without its bristles
Refs without whistles,

A glacier without ice
Ludo without dice
A chair without a seat
Steps without feet,

A hat without a head
A toaster without bread
A riddle without a clue
Me without you.

Used Furniture
Judith W. Steinbergh

Sometimes we all go meet at the Used Furniture,
we can take a seat, right outside of the Used Furniture,
Mr. Lewis sets those kitchen chairs,
right out in the city air,
red plastic with shiny chrome,
it almost feels like home, at the Used Furniture.

You can play a little gin at the Used Furniture,
hold your cards close to your chin at the Used Furniture,
formica table on the walk,
some old uncles come and talk,
Jimmy whittles with his knife,
Giovanni's throwing dice at the Used Furniture.

You can play a little house at the Used Furniture.
Curl up on a fuzzy couch at the Used Furniture.
He's got a fancy mirror, a double bed,
some old books, already read,
You pick out some things you like,
imagine how you'll live your life at the Used Furniture.

Mr. Lewis sits on down and jokes,
he likes his furniture used by folks.

The Vacuum Cleaner's Swallowed Will
X. J. Kennedy

The vacuum cleaner's swallowed Will.
He's vanished. What a drag!
Still, we can do without him till
It's time to change the bag.

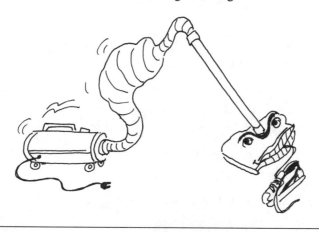

You can't write without reading, so read everything you can find by writers whose work you love. Don't be afraid to imitate them if you want to. Eventually you will come to sound not like them anymore, but like yourself. —X. J. Kennedy

V V V V V V V V V V

VAMPIRE POEM
Lois Simmie

If you think
Mosquito bites pain ya,
Be glad you don't live
In Transylvania.

VUlTURES
Beverly McLoughland

Perched high along the railing
Of a tall blue water tower
Are a dozen turkey vultures
Hunched and silent, ever staring
Every day I come to watch them
Waiting breathless for the moment
When they all take off like eagles
Circling slowly, high and higher.
And I love to watch them soaring
And the beauty of their black wings
As they go about their business
Disregarding reputation.

Wishing
Lois Simmie

I wish my hair had some curly
And my clothes had some frilly and swirly;
That my nose wasn't runny
And my ears weren't funny,
That my name wasn't Alvina Shirley.

I wish that my room had some neat,
And my legs didn't have so much feet;
That my father could cook,
That my line had a hook,
That my red skirt had more than one pleat.

I wish that my cat had a tail,
I wish that my school had no fail;
That my yard had a pool
And my toad had a stool,
That my brother was locked up in jail.

I wish that my eyes were true blue
And my tooth wasn't loose when I chew;

That my bike had a chain,
That my head had a brain,

I wish I was somebody new.

Winter evening
Nicholas A. Virgilio

leaving father's footprints:
> I sink into deep snow.

X is for x
William Jay Smith

And X marks the spot
On the rug in the parlor,
The sand in the lot,
Where once you were standing,
And now you are not.
x is for **x**

Be patient, work hard, accept only the best from yourself, and, like all true poets, love and respect our great heritage, our language. —William Jay Smith

---

Yak
William Jay Smith

The long-haired Yak has long black hair,
He lets it grow—he doesn't care.
He lets it grow and grow and grow,
He lets it trail along the stair.
Does he ever go to the barbershop? NO!
How wild and woolly and devil-may-care
A long-haired Yak with long black hair
Would look when perched in a barber chair!

Z Z Z Z Z Z Z Z **Z**

Zebra
Bobbi Katz

Zebra, zebra—
wild and free
once you traveled
the African plains.
Caught and caged,
your freedom's gone,
but your wild beauty remains

Zebra, zebra—
one day soon
we'll gallop away
to the sea.
I won't keep you
in a cage.
Together, we both will be
free!

Further Reading

Humorous Poetry

Kennedy, X. J. *Fresh Brats*. McElderry, 1990.

Lewis, J. Patrick. *A Hippopotamusn't*. Dial, 1990.

————. *Two-Legged, Four-Legged, No-Legged Rhymes*. Knopf, 1991.

Merriam, Eve. *Chortles: New and Selected Wordplay Poems*. Morrow, 1989.

Moss, Jeff. *The Butterfly Jar*. Bantam, 1989.

————. *The Other Side of the Door*. Bantam, 1991.

Prelutsky, Jack. *Poems of A. Nonny Mouse*. Knopf, 1989.

Smith, William Jay. *Laughing Time: Collected Nonsense*. Farrar, 1990.

Nature Poetry

Booth, David, ed. *Voices on the Wind: Poems for All Seasons*. Morrow, 1990.

Frank, Josette, ed. *Snow toward Evening: A Year in a River Valley*. Dial, 1990.

Heard, Georgia. *Creatures of Earth, Sea, and Sky*. Boyds Mills, 1992.

Hubbell, Patricia. *The Tiger Brought Pink Lemonade*. Atheneum, 1989.

Lewis, J. Patrick. *Earth Verse and Water Rhymes*. Atheneum, 1991.

Singer, Marilyn. *Turtle in July*. Macmillan, 1989.

General Anthologies

Larrick, Nancy, ed. *To the Moon and Back: A Collection of Poems*. Delacorte, 1991.

Philip, Neil, ed. *A New Treasury of Poetry*. Blackie, 1990.

Prelutsky, Jack, ed. *The Random House Book of Poetry for Children*. Random House, 1983.

de Regniers, Beatrice Schenk, et al., eds. *Sing a Song of Popcorn*. Scholastic, 1988.

Slier, Deborah, ed. *Make a Joyful Sound: Poems for Children by African-American Poets*. Checkerboard, 1991.

Specialized Anthologies

Bober, Natalie S., ed. *Let's Pretend: Poems of Flight and Fancy*. Viking, 1989.

Clark, Emma Chichester, ed. *I Never Saw a Purple Cow*. Little, Brown, 1991.

Janeczko, Paul B., ed. *The Place My Words Are Looking For*. Bradbury, 1990.

Marcus, Leonard S., and Amy Schwartz, eds. *Mother Goose's Little Misfortunes*. Bradbury, 1990.

Prelutsky, Jack, ed. *For Laughing Out Loud: Poems to Tickle Your Funnybone*. Knopf, 1991.

Sneve, Virginia Driving Hawk, ed. *Dancing Teepees: Poems of American Indian Youth*. Holiday House, 1989.

Steele, Susanna, and Morag Styles, eds. *Mother Gave a Shout: Poems by Women and Girls*. Volcano, 1991.

Individual Poets

Adoff, Arnold. *Chocolate Dreams*. Lothrop, 1989.

Edwards, Richard. *A Mouse in My Roof*. Delacorte, 1988.

Greenfield, Eloise. *Nathaniel Talking*. Black Butterfly, 1988.

———. *Under the Sunday Tree*. Harper, 1988.

Joseph, Lynn. *Coconut Kind of Day: Island Poems*. Lothrop, 1990.

Livingston, Myra Cohn. *Birthday Poems*. Holiday House, 1989.

Roth, Susan L. *Gypsy Bird Song*. Farrar, 1991.

Soto, Gary. *A Fire in My Hands*. Scholastic, 1990.

Single-Story Poems

Fields, Julia. *The Green Lion of Zion Street*. McElderry, 1988.

Janeczko, Paul B. *Brickyard Summer*. Orchard, 1989.

———. *Stardust Otel*. Orchard, 1993.

Rylant, Cynthia. *Waiting to Waltz: A Childhood*. Bradbury, 1984.

Salter, Mary Jo. *The Moon Comes Home*. Knopf, 1989.

Seabrooke, Brenda. *Judy Scuppernong*. Dutton, 1990.

Acknowledgments

Permission to reprint copyrighted poems is gratefully acknowledged to the following:

Atheneum Publishers, a division of Simon & Schuster Children's Books, for "Prayer for Reptiles" and "Concrete Mixers" by Patricia Hubbell from *8 A.M. Shadows* by Patricia Hubbell, Copyright © 1993 by Patricia Hubbell. "Harvey" by Judith Viorst from *If I Were in Charge of the World and Other Worries* by Judith Viorst, Copyright © 1981 by Judith Viorst.

Jean Balderston, for "Snake Date" from *Light: A Quarterly of Humorous, Occasional, Ephemeral & Light Verse*, Copyright © 1993 by Jean Balderston.

Boyds Mills Press, for "Dragonfly" by Georgia Heard from *Creatures of Earth, Sea, and Sky* by Georgia Heard, Copyright © 1992 by Georgia Heard. "Tugboat at Daybreak" by Lillian Morrison from *Whistling the Morning In* by Lillian Morrison, Copyright © 1992 by Lillian Morrison.

Gwendolyn Brooks, for "Building" from *The Near-Johannesburg Boy* by Gwendolyn Brooks, Copyright © 1991 by Gwendolyn Brooks.

Siv Cedering, for "Returning the Red Gloves" from *Color Poems* by Siv Cedering, Copyright © 1978 by Siv Cedering.

Don Congdon Associates, Inc., for "The Best Meal I Ever Had Anywhere" by Ellen Gilchrist, Copyright © 1988 by Ellen Gilchrist.

117

Index

126

128